JAKE

GRA

SIXTH MAN SURPRISE

STONE ARCH BOOKS
a capstone imprint

JAKE MADDOX
GRAPHIC NOVELS

Published by Stone Arch Books,
an imprint of Capstone.
1710 Roe Crest Drive
North Mankato, Minnesota 56003
capstonepub.com

Library of Congress Cataloging-in-Publication Data
Names: Maddox, Jake, author. | San Juan, Mel Joy, illustrator. | Pryor, Shawn, author.
Title: Sixth man surprise / Jake Maddox; [text by] Shawn Pryor; [illustrated by] Mel Joy San Juan.
Description: North Mankato, Minnesota : Stone Arch Books, 2023. | Series: Jake Maddox graphic novels | Audience: Ages 8-12. | Audience: Grades 4-6. | Summary: Thirteen-year-old Devante Briggs loves basketball, but now he is the sixth man off the bench for his school team, putting up with the snide remarks of some of the other players—until an outbreak of food poisoning gives him his chance to show off his skills.
Identifiers: LCCN 2022029405 (print) | LCCN 2022029406 (ebook) | ISBN 9781666341263 (hardcover) | ISBN 9781666341300 (paperback) | ISBN 9781666341317 (pdf) | ISBN 9781666341331 (kindle edition)
Subjects: LCSH: Basketball stories. | Basketball—Comic books, strips, etc. | African American boys—Comic books, strips, etc. | African American boys—Juvenile fiction. | Teamwork (Sports)—Juvenile fiction. | Teamwork (Sports)—Comic books, strips, etc. | Self-confidence—Juvenile fiction. | Self-confidence—Comic books, strips, etc. | Graphic novels. | CYAC: Graphic novels. | Basketball—Fiction. | African Americans—Fiction. | Teamwork (Sports)—Fiction. | Self-confidence—Fiction. | LCGFT: Sports fiction. | Graphic novels.
Classification: LCC PZ7.7.M33 Si 2023 (print) | LCC PZ7.7.M33 (ebook) | DDC 741.5/973—dc23/eng/20220711
LC record available at https://lccn.loc.gov/2022029405
LC ebook record available at https://lccn.loc.gov/2022029406

Editor: Amanda Robbins
Designer: Heidi Thompson
Production Specialist: Tori Abraham

Design Elements
Shutterstock: orbcat

Printed and bound in China. 5828

SIXTH MAN SURPRISE

Text by Shawn Pryor
Art by Mel Joy San Juan
Cover art by Berenice Muñiz

CAST OF CHARACTERS

Devante Briggs

Adam

Coach Clark

Michael

Mr. and Mrs.
Briggs

Kelly Briggs

Terry, Martheus, Jordan

Skylar

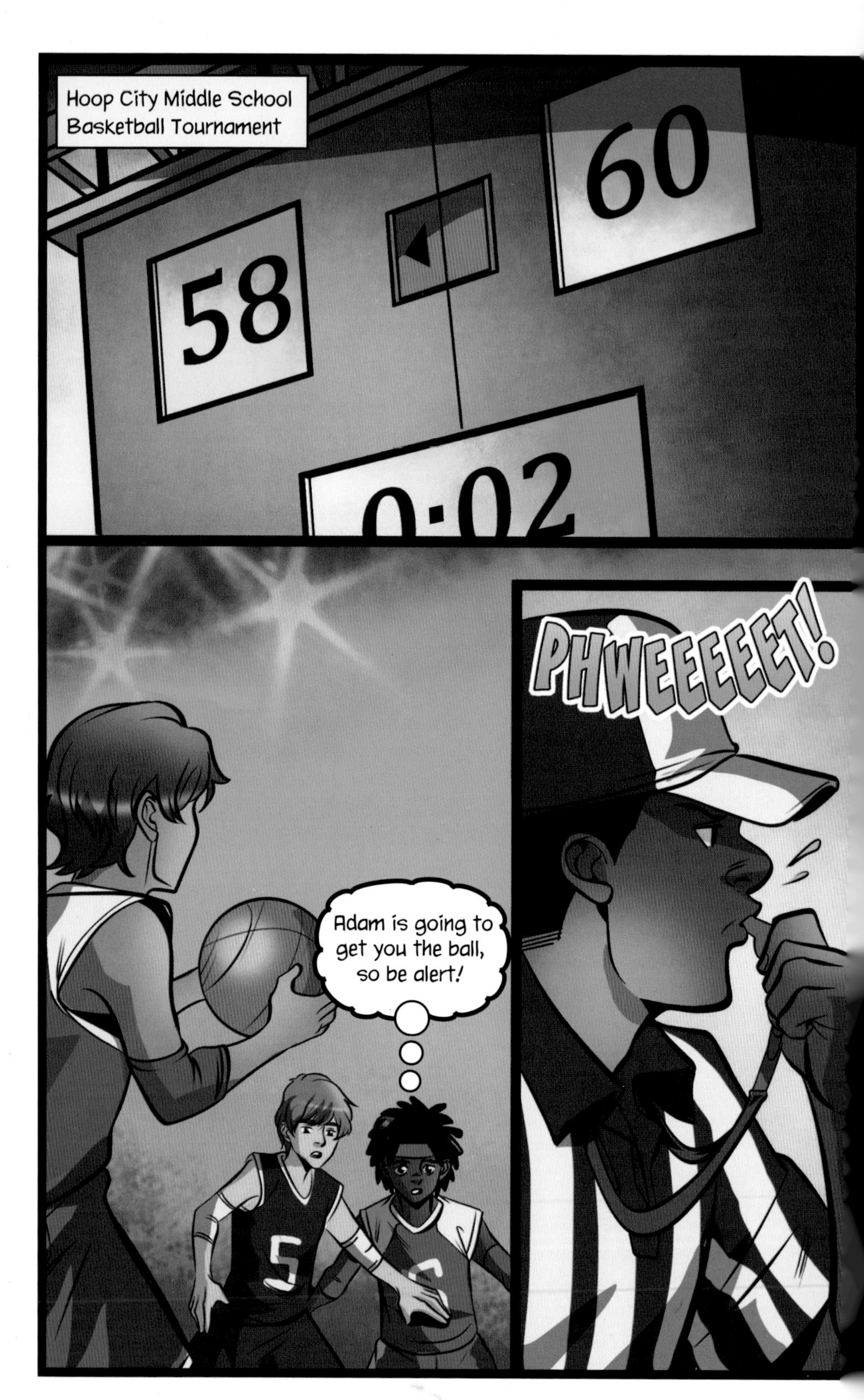
Hoop City Middle School
Basketball Tournament
58
60
0:02
PHWEEEEET!
Adam is going to get you the ball, so be alert!
5

Get ready for the pass, Devante.
BOUNCE!

I never thought I'd be the one taking the shot—

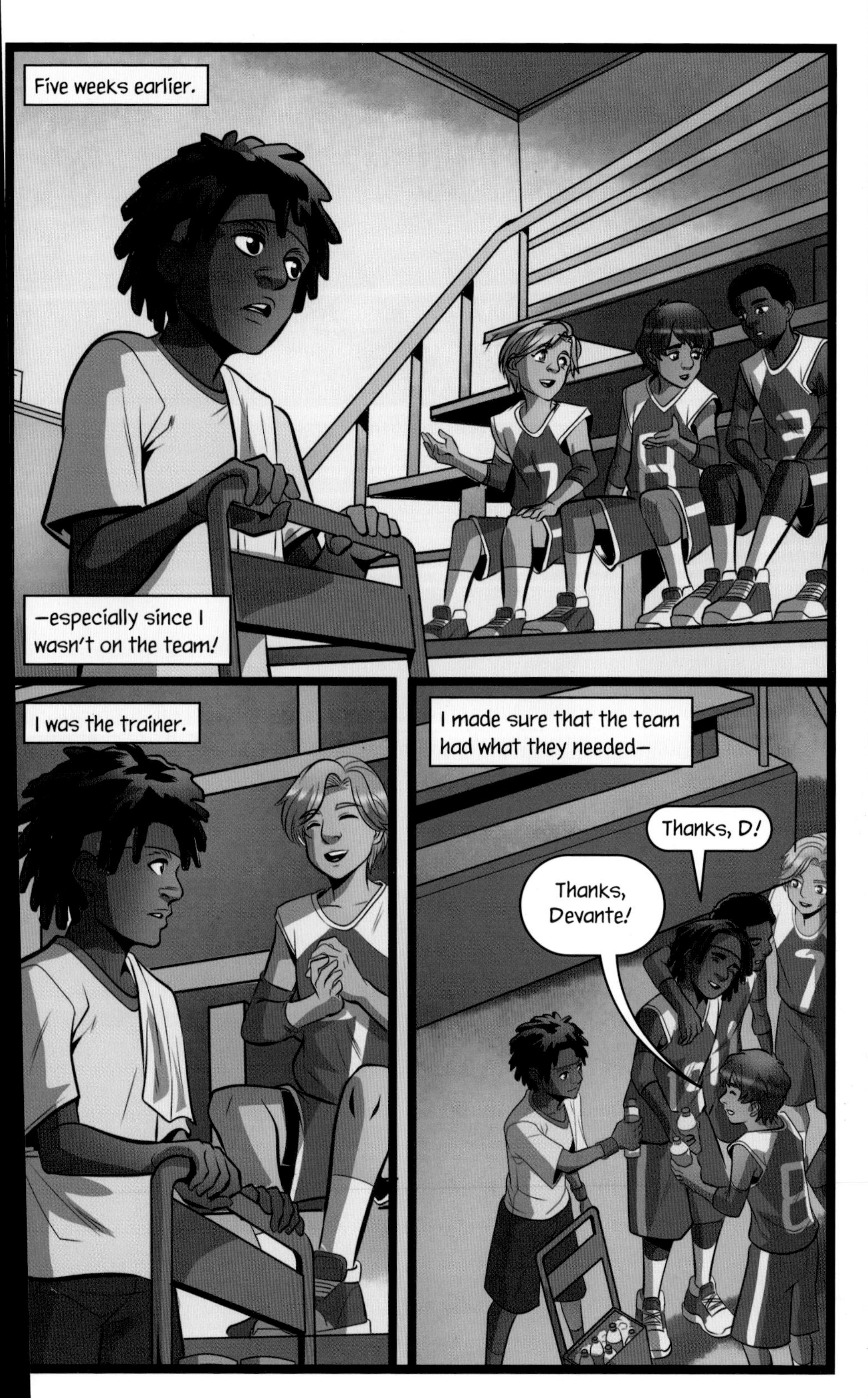
Five weeks earlier.
—especially since I wasn't on the team!
I was the trainer.
I made sure that the team had what they needed—
Thanks, D!
Thanks, Devante!

—even though some of the players couldn't have cared less.
PLAPP!
Thanks, scrub!
Don't treat Devante that way, Michael.
He's just a dorky trainer, Adam. He's not important.
SIGH

I've loved basketball since I was little.

02
My sister Kelly plays professionally, and I want to follow in her footsteps.

So I practiced . . .

I led my sixth grade team in scoring too.
. . . and I played in rec leagues.
Before seventh grade tryouts, I worked out with my sister as much as possible.
Show me what you got, Devante!
I was ready to do whatever it took to make the team.

But I got a bad case of the flu the week of tryouts.
I was so disappointed. I missed my shot to make the team.

Still, I wanted to be a part of the team.
Hey Coach, I heard you need a trainer.
Yes. We need someone to keep the water bottles full and the uniforms and towels clean.
I'm your guy, Coach. Count me in.

It was a lot of work.

But it was worth it.
I got to sit in during practices and games.

And while doing my duties as a trainer, I learned how the team ran their offense and defense.

Sometimes Coach Clark would let me practice with the team when they needed an extra person to run drills.

HEY!

Hey Devante!
Hey Adam!

Here are some leftover towels from practice.
Thanks.

You got lucky with those steals today, dork.
Just because Coach lets you pretend to be on the team sometimes—
Doesn't mean that you're a part of this team.
That's enough, guys!
You're just a scrubby trainer.
Well, this scrubby trainer stole the ball from you five times today!
Every single person on this team is important, including the trainer!
Whatever. Just because you're the captain doesn't mean you're the boss of me.
C'mon guys, let's get out of here.

You okay?
Yeah, I guess. What's his deal, anyway?
I wish I knew.
Practice is over, but I'm going to work on some drills and extra shooting. You game?
Yeah! Let me start this laundry first!
Working on my skills with Adam after practice is a lot of fun.

And it will get me ready for next year's tryouts.
I also get to work on my long-range game.
That's fifteen threes in a row!
You keep getting better, Devante! Way to go!
Thanks!
Adam is a good friend.

You're a lock for the eighth grade team next year.
You think so?
No doubt! You're more than just a trainer, dude.
Hey! Are you two going to be in the gym all day?
Hey Skylar!
Let's go get something to eat!
Sounds good to me!
Skylar is my best friend.

Who's your next game against?
We're going up against the Greenbrook County Giants. They're tough on defense.
And they're undefeated. It's been year since we've beat them.
Yeah, but we'll be able to hang with them.

Yeah, and we've had great practices this week. I think we can win.
Don't worry, I'll be dishing out water bottles and towels during time-outs as if they were assists!
Hey!
I ran out of fries, so I *assisted* myself to yours.
Ha Ha Ha

A few days later, we had our big game against the Greenbrook County Giants.
But there was a problem.
Bad news, guys. A bunch of kids got food poisoning from lunch today, including seven of our players.
That's why I never eat the school's meatloaf.
Not the time for jokes, Martheus.

Sorry, Coach.
But that means we'll only have four players!
Greenbrook County is going to wear us out.
We're going to get creamed!
I've got it!

Coach, let Devante play with us tonight!
Me? For real?
You gotta be kidding me!
Well, I guess the trainer is better than nobody.
Coach, Devante has been at every practice. He knows how we run our offense and defense.
He does practice with us sometimes, Coach.

Plus, Devante and I do drills and shooting together after practice. He's got the skills.
I guess I'd rather have five players on the court than four.
Hmm. Well . . .
Suit up, Devante! You know where the extra uniforms are.
Are you serious?!?!
I won't let you guys down!
Just do your best, man.

This is going to be such a joke.
Skylar and my parents come to all the games. They like to support the team.
No way!
Wait a minute! Are you seeing what I'm seeing?
It can't be!
Tonight, they were in for a surprise.
I heard a bunch of kids got food poisoning today. I bet it was them!
But where is the rest of the team?
Devante is playing tonight!

They've only got five players!
This is going to be a breeze!
They're going to be worn out after the first quarter.
THUMP!
Don't screw this up, trainer.
I won't let them get to me.
I'll show them what I can do on the court.

First Quarter
What the???

Did you see that pass?!?!
My baby did that! Get Kelly on video chat, she's got to see this!
Okay, okay!
We had Greenbrook on their toes in the first quarter.

SWISHHHH!
Wow! I wasn't expecting this!
Nice three-pointer, Devante!
Thanks!
We were up by five at the end of the quarter!
But without any bench players, we were exhausted.

Coach told us to play zone defense instead of man-to-man.
Which led to us getting a lot of turnovers on defense!

In the first half, we did all we could.
And while we kept Greenbrook on their toes—
Nice layup, Jordan!
—It wasn't enough.

Guys, I'm wiped.
I haven't run this much in my entire life.
At halftime, we were only down by five.
We got this, guys. They have a whole squad and we've still got them on their heels.
Jordan's right. If we continue to give it our all, we can win. Wildcats on three: 1-2-3—
WILDCATS!

Hey, Devante!
Look, I don't want any troub—
You're balling out there. Keep it up!
Oh. Thanks!
Let's go win this game!

We gave it all we had in the second half.
But eventually, we ran out of steam.
We started making mistakes.
We tried to keep the game close.

I even made five three-pointers in the second half!

I struggled with my free throws, though.

In the end, Greenbrook was too much for us.
GO TEAM!!
WILDCATS
#11
65
75
00:00
We lost.
Good game.
Good game.
You guys were tough!
Thanks!
Yeah, there's no way we would've lasted on the court with just five players!
Today was Devante's first game. He's our trainer!
If it wasn't for Devante, we would've only had four players!
No way!
That's awesome!

Even though we lost, it felt good to be on the court.
You did great, man!
I'm so proud of you, Devante!
Hey, someone else wants to talk to you!
Hey, little brother! When did you get a three-point jump shot?
You saw me play?
Saw? Me and the team watched the whole game!
You all played your butts off!
You've got better handles than your sister, Devante!
Hey now!

We're proud of you, little bro! Love you!
Love you too!
I didn't want the day to end.
But tomorrow, it was back to being a trainer.
It was fun while it lasted.
Midville Middle School, a few days later.

Welp, back to handing out towels and water bottles. Thanks for getting Coach to let me play, even if it was only for one game.

Of course, man. I just wish you could always play with us.

Hey y'all!
Devante, Coach Clark is looking for you!
Me? Why?
I don't know, but he said it's important.
He probably forgot to clean the water bottles.

I heard that they let the trainer play. And just like I thought, you all lost.
I knew you were just a scrub.
I'm not a scrub, and my name is **Devante**!
Chill, Michael. We may have lost, but Devante was our top scorer!
You're taking his side now?

Whatever.
Later, losers.
I don't know why he hates me so much.
So I went to see the coach . . .
Jordan said you wanted to see me?
Yep. Come on in.
You did one heck of a job on the court the other day.
Thanks, Coach.

How would you like to officially be on the team?
Really? Are you serious right now!?
With the whole team back, I can't guarantee anything. But prove yourself in practice, and you can earn playing time.
Count me in, Coach! Thank you!

I couldn't believe it. I was really on the team now!
It was so awesome!

For the next couple of games, I mostly sat on the bench.

But later on, Coach made me the team's sixth man.
Devante, go in for Michael.
Which means I come off the bench and provide a spark for the team.
Not everyone on the team liked my new role.

But any time my number was called—

—I gave everything I had.

I was on cloud nine. Until—

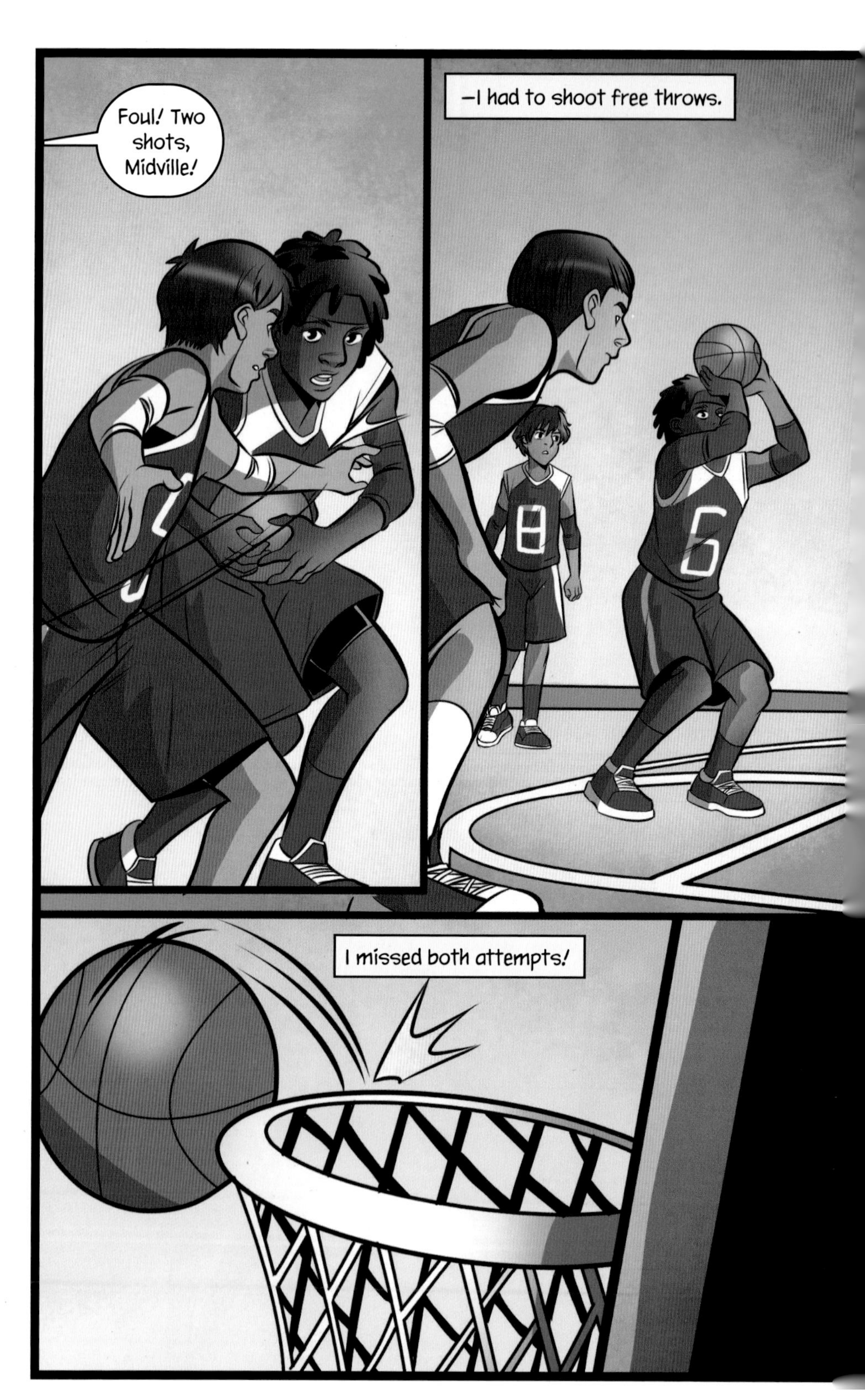
Foul! Two shots, Midville!
—I had to shoot free throws.
I missed both attempts!

And at the next game—
—I missed five free throws, and I even air-balled one!
It was embarrassing!
But the worst was the last game of the season.
If we win this game against Taft, we're a lock for the middle school tournament.
If we lose, we're in a play-in game to get into the tournament.
A play-in game meant we would have a must-win extra game in order to make the tourney.
We have to win this game.

I came off the bench and was a scoring machine!
This was going to be an easy win!

Foul him whenever he gets the ball! He can't shoot free throws!
But Taft's coach had other plans.

His plan worked.

In the second quarter I missed eight free throws!

Coach had to bench me for the rest of the game.
Things got worse after the game.
Great. Thanks to the scrub, we gotta play an extra game to make the playoffs.
60
62
00:00
We lost by two points. If I could've hit a couple of free throws, we would've won.

Lay off Devante, Michael! He's not the only one who made mistakes today.
Quit sticking up for him!

I knew the trainer would end up hurting us in the long run.

My name is Devante!

Knock it off you two!
We win as a team, and we lose as a team.
If we don't support each other as a team, we can kiss the tournament goodbye.
Hey, where are you going?
Devante???
I didn't mean to blow off Adam, but I needed to cool off.

Several days later . . .
Where's Devante? I haven't seen him at lunch the last four days. He's not answering my texts, either.
He feels he let you all down because the team lost the last game.
He's been skipping lunch to go to the gym and practice his free throws.

Hey, where are you going, Michael?
Okay, just focus and concentrate. You can do it.
NO!
Why can't I make a free throw!?!?

Whoa! That's no way to treat a basketball, dude.
What do you want?
I'm not here to start a fight. I know I've been a jerk to you.
You may not believe it, but I'm sorry.
Truth is, I'm jealous. I played against your team in summer league last year. I know you're good. And since we play the same position, I thought that you might take my spot.

Coach Clark is right: We win as a team, and we lose as a team. I want to help you.
How?
I may not be better than you at three-pointers, but I can do free throws.
Stop shooting with just your arms. You need to use your whole body.
Eyes on the basket, hands on the ball, use your whole body, and follow through.
Just like that. You try.

Remember, eyes, hands, body, follow through.
Sigh.
That's okay, try it again!
I did it! I did it!

I kept using Michael's free throw method. I missed a few.
But I started making more shots than I missed!
And all it took to make it happen was a little teamwork.

Now, back to the beginning of my story!
PHWEEEEET!
OW!

0:00
Foul, Battlebirds!
Wildcats shoot three free throws!
You okay?
Yeah, but I missed.
That's okay, you've got three free throws! We only need two to make it to overtime.
Or all three to win.
You got this, man. We believe in you.

It's just you, the ball, and the basket.
Eyes, hands, body, follow through.
SWISHHHH!
Do it again.

WHOOSH!
One more and we win!
You got this, D!
Last one.

This one's for the win.

11
2

You did it! We won!

From trainer, to sixth man, to game-winning free throws!
I couldn't have done it without you!
1-2-3-
WILDCATS!
THE END

VISUAL DISCUSSION QUESTIONS

1. Even though Devante wasn't on the team, he still wanted to support it. Why do you think that is? What does that say about Devante, and how do you think he is feeling in this panel?

2. Sound effects can bring a story to life. The text reads "PHWEEEEEET!", but that nonsense word is just a symbol for the sound a whistle makes. When you read it, what do you hear in your mind?

3. In graphic novels, the art can often show a character's emotions better than words. What do you think Michael is feeling in this scene?

4. Look at the sequence of panels above. Why do you think the artist chose to show the action this way? What do you think the characters are feeling in these moments?

LEARN MORE ABOUT BASKETBALL

James Naismith is known as the founder of basketball. He created the sport in 1891. Naismith was a gym teacher. He wrote the first rule book for basketball and created the University of Kansas basketball program.

Back in the 1890s, basketball was played with a soccer ball and peach baskets. Every time a team scored, the referees would have to get a ladder to get the ball out of the basket in order for the game to continue. Finally, in the early 1900s, string baskets were finally brought in.

Basketball became an official Olympic sport in 1936 at the Berlin Summer Games.

From 1967 to 1976, the slam dunk was banned from collegiate basketball due to committees feeling that dunking was not a shot that required skill.

The first use of the three-point line in basketball was in 1961, in the American Basketball League (ABL).

The first three point shot made in the history of the NBA (National Basketball Association) was made by guard Chris Ford of the Boston Celtics in 1979.

The most total points ever scored in a professional basketball game is 370. The Detroit Pistons defeated the Denver Nuggets in triple overtime, 186 to 184 in 1983.

The height of the basketball rim for the NBA, Women's National Basketball Association (WNBA), the International Basketball Federation (FIBA), and the National Collegiate Athletic Association (NCAA) is 10 feet (3 meters).

BASKETBALL TERMS YOU SHOULD KNOW

air ball—a shot that misses and doesn't touch the rim, net, or backboard at all

assist—an offensive pass to another player that leads to a made basket

backboard—the piece of wood or fiberglass that the rim attaches to in order to play basketball

double dribble—when a player dribbles the ball, stops, and starts to dribble the ball again

free throw—a free shot or shots given to a player after a foul, or technical foul

layup—a close shot taken at the hoop, normally as a player is moving toward the basket

man-to-man—when each player on the defensive side of the ball guards one person on the opposing team

rebound—when a player from a team retrieves the ball from a missed shot

swish—when the ball avoids the rim during a shot and touches nothing but the net, making a "swish" sound

turnover—when the offense loses possession of the ball by making an offensive foul, gets the ball stolen from them, or makes the ball go out-of-bounds

zone—when players on defense guard a specific area of the court instead of a player on the other team

GLOSSARY

defense (DEE-fenss)—when a team tries to stop points from being scored

drill (DRIL)—to practice skills over and over

league (LEEG)—a group of sports teams that play against each other

offense (aw-FENSS)—when a team tries to score points

officially (uh-FISH-uhl-ee)—having been approved by those in authority

professionally (pruh-FESH-uh-nuhl-ee)—when someone makes money by doing an activity that other people might do without pay

tournament (TUR-nuh-muhnt)—a series of matches between several players or teams, ending in one winner

undefeated (un-duh-FEET-uhd)—having never lost in competition

ABOUT THE AUTHOR

SHAWN PRYOR'S (he/him) work includes the middle-grade graphic novel series Cash and Carrie (Action Lab Entertainment), the 2019 Glyph Nominated sports graphic novel *Force* (Action Lab Entertainment), several books for Capstone's Jake Maddox Sports and Adventure series, and the Kids Sports Stories series. In his free time, Shawn enjoys reading, cooking, listening to streaming music playlists, and talking about why Zack from the Mighty Morphin Power Rangers is the greatest superhero of all-time.

ABOUT THE ARTISTS

Mel Joy San Juan is a full-time illustrator from Cavite, Philippines. She started illustrating various comic books and manga upon joining Glasshouse Graphics during her teenage years. She is best known for her graphic novel illustration, such as Sherrilyn Kenyon's Dark Hunter series, *Call of Duty: Recon for Activision*, and other independent comic books. She is currently happily working on a comic book with the help of her sidekick, Maddie.

Berenice Muñiz is a graphic designer and illustrator from Monterrey, Mexico. She has done work for publicity agencies, art exhibitions, and even created her own webcomic. These days, Berenice is devoted to illustrating comics as part of the Graphikslava crew.

READ THEM ALL!

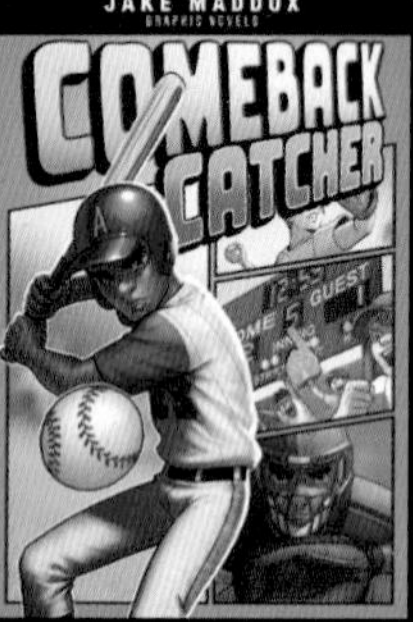

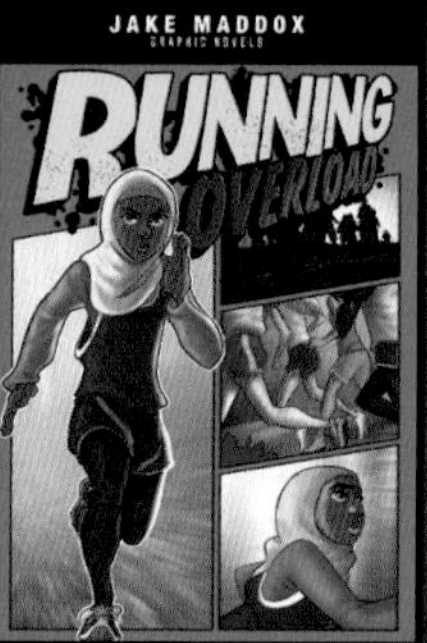

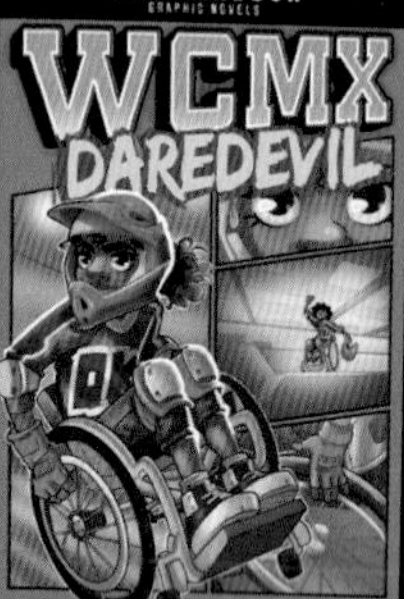